Haircut Day at the Poodle Salon

Janet Charlebois

Max

COPPER

MILLION

- Book 2 -

This book is dedicated to:

Rich, Joel & Becky

Mom & Dad

The Charlebois Family

Jim & family

The Sitter, McCaughan Family

My Friends

All of Max's readers

My dearest Max

So very grateful for all of you!

Today, Max has an appointment to have a haircut at the Poodle Salon.

Max doesn't like having a haircut! He always hides on haircut day! Jannie will have to find Max.

Jannie starts looking around the house for Max.

IS  IN THE KITCHEN?

Jannie can't find him in the kitchen!

IS Max IN THE BEDROOM?

Jannie can't find Max in the bedroom!

IS Max IN THE BATHROOM?

Jannie can't find Max in the bathroom!

Where could Max be?

Jannie said, "Maybe Max is in the family room. It is dark in here. I will turn the lamp on." Jannie felt something soft and fuzzy under the lampshade - **Zap!**

"OH

THERE YOU ARE!"

"COME ON BOY, IT'S TIME FOR YOUR HAIRCUT. LET'S GET YOU OUT TO THE CAR."

SAID, "HERE WE ARE,
MAX. WE ARE AT THE
POODLE SALON!"

Jannie gave Max to the friendly dog groomer and said, "Just a little trim for Max today please."

The dog groomer told Jannie to come back in one hour to pick up Max.

"SEE YOU SOON, MAX".

Jannie waved at Max and left the Poodle Salon. She had some shopping to do.

Jannie went back to the Poodle Salon one hour later. She asked the groomer at the counter if Max was ready.

"One moment please," said the lady.

Jannie sat in the waiting room.

SHE WAS EXCITED TO SEE

Max!

When the groomer came back, she put a funny-looking dog on the counter.

"HERE HE IS," SHE SAID.

SCREECHED,

"THAT'S NOT MY DOG!
I WANT MY DOG!
WHERE IS MAX?

MAX, WHERE ARE YOU?"

The groomer said to Jannie, "This is your dog-this **is** Max!"

Max was poofy and had blue bows on his ears and the top of his head.

WAS **NOT** HAPPY!

When Max and Jannie got into the car, Jannie said to Max, "I will make you your favourite dinner when we get home."

LOVES SPAGHETTI AND MEATBALLS!

While Jannie started dinner, Max ran to his piano. Playing piano always makes Max happy.

"The Wonder Dog Boy...the Wonder Dog Boy...he is Max, the Wonder Dog Boy...he's scared of haircuts, he's just a cute Mutt, he is Max, the Wonder Dog Boy!"

Max felt much better after playing his song on the piano.

He also knew that his fur would grow back soon. He would look more like his cute, shaggy self in a week or two!

MaX

RAN TO THE KITCHEN
TO DIG IN TO THE
DELICIOUS SPAGHETTI
AND MEATBALLS THAT
JANNIE MADE FOR HIM.

THE END

IF YOU LIKE

MaX

AND

JaNNie's

SONG, GO TO MAX'S FACEBOOK
PAGE **f** Max Copper Million
TO HELP THEM WITH NEW
WORDS FOR THE NEXT BOOK.

Just fill in the blanks!

"The Wonder Dog Boy...the Wonder Dog Boy...
he is Max, the Wonder Dog Boy... he _____ -
_____, he _____ - _____, he is Max, the
Wonder Dog Boy!"

Your ideas could be chosen to
be written in the next book of

THE GREAT
ADVENTURES OF

COPPER MILLION!

If your words for the song
are selected for an upcoming
book, you will have a chance to
have your name printed in that
book and sent a free copy!

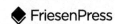 FriesenPress

Suite 300 - 990 Fort St
Victoria, BC, V8V 3K2
Canada

www.friesenpress.com

ISBN
978-1-5255-1627-6 (Hardback)
978-1-5255-1628-3 (Paperback)
978-1-5255-1629-0 (eBook)

1. JUVENILE FICTION, ANIMALS, DOGS

Distributed to the trade by The Ingram Book Company

CPSIA information can be obtained
at www.ICGtesting.com
Printed in the USA
LVOW06s0454031217
557932LV00007B/10/P